Also Available:

THE BARE BUM GANG AND
THE FOOTBALL FACE-OFF

THE BARE BUM GANG BATTLE
THE DOGSNATCHERS

Coming Soon:

THE BARE BUM GANG
AND THE HOLY GRAIL

www.barebumgang.com

THE BARE BUM GANG
and the
Valley of Doom

ANTHONY McGOWAN

Illustrated by Frances Castle

RED FOX

THE BARE BUM GANG AND THE VALLEY OF DOOM
A RED FOX BOOK 978 1 862 30388 1

First published in Great Britain by Red Fox,
an imprint of Random House Children's Publishers UK
A Random House Group Company

This edition published 2009

5 7 9 10 8 6

Text copyright © Anthony McGowan, 2009
Illustrations copyright © Frances Castle, 2009

The right of Anthony McGowan to be identified as the author
of this work has been asserted in accordance with the Copyright,
Designs and Patents Act 1988.

Set in Bembo MT Schoolbook

Red Fox Books are published by Random House Children's Publishers UK,
61–63 Uxbridge Road, London W5 5SA

www.**randomhousechildrens**.co.uk
www.randomhouse.co.uk

Addresses for companies within The Random House Group Limited can be
found at: www.randomhouse.co.uk/offices.htm

THE RANDOM HOUSE GROUP Limited Reg. No. 954009

A CIP catalogue record for this book is available from the British Library.

The Random House Group Limited supports The Forest Stewardship
Council® (FSC®), the leading international forest-certification organisation.
Our books carrying the FSC label are printed on FSC®-certified paper.
FSC is the only forest-certification scheme supported by the leading
environmental organisations, including Greenpeace. Our
paper procurement policy can be found at
www.randomhouse.co.uk/environment

MIX
Paper from
responsible sources
FSC® C016897

Printed and bound in Great Britain by Clays Ltd, St Ives PLC

To Gabriel McGowan,
coolest boy in Year 5

Chapter One

THE RAID

The path through the Valley of Doom was narrow, and the dark, humid jungle closed in all around us. Sweat poured down my face, stinging my eyes. Exotic birds screeched in the trees, and I could hear the sound of giant, blood-sucking leeches squirming their way towards us through the undergrowth.

We were deep in enemy territory, so we had to keep absolute radio silence, and if anyone burped or farted they had to do it really, really, really quietly.

The mission had been planned with the utmost care and attention. We were equipped

with the latest hi-tech gear. I had my best binoculars, a magnifying glass, a bow and arrow, one of the walkie-talkies, and a cheese sandwich. The Moan (Phillip) had his cowboy pistols (with caps, so they made a good loud bang), a spear, the lemonade bottle filled with Special Mixture Number Seven, and a sausage roll. Noah, our Gang Doctor, didn't believe in weapons so he carried the funnel, a banana and six little cartons of orange juice.

Jennifer, the Moan's sister, was also unarmed, but that was because she was lethal in Ninja-style hand-to-hand combat

and all she needed was her tracksuit. And her hands. Hand-to-hand combat is hard if you haven't got any hands – say if they were eaten by piranha fish while you dangled them over the side of your boat on the Amazon river.

Jennifer had the balloons in her bum bag. She hadn't brought any food supplies, but I said she could have half of my cheese sandwich, because I'm so nice.

Jamie, our Gang General, was wearing his camouflaged commando trousers, which looked really cool. He'd also blackened his face with burnt cork. You do that so the enemy can't see you at night. The trouble was it was half past ten in the morning, so he looked a bit silly, although none of us had the heart to tell him. As well as his black face and combat trousers, Jamie had the other walkie-talkie.

The walkie-talkies would have been brilliant for a secret mission like this, except that the batteries had run out. The Moan said that meant they were about as useful as a chocolate teapot, but then I pointed out that a chocolate teapot was actually very useful indeed because you could eat it. In fact it was miles better than a real teapot, because we don't even like tea.

I suppose I'd better explain the balloons and the funnel and the Special Mixture Number Seven. But to explain that I'll have to explain why we were on the mission in the first place.

Chapter Two

THE MYSTERY BOY

Jennifer, who is a girl and therefore has a very acute sense of smell, was the first to notice it.

'Poooooooooooh!' she screamed, one evening when we met up in the den after school. 'Smell that, Ludo!'

'What?' I asked.

'Weeeeeeeeeeeeeeee!'

'Eh?'

'It smells of wee in here. Absolutely stinks.'

And it did. We all agreed. Our den smelled of wee.

'I think I'm sitting on a wet patch,' said Noah, on the verge of tears. We'd all got used to Noah being on the brink of tears. He wasn't a complete cry-baby, just a bit of a wuss.

'Let's get out of here,' I said.

So, Noah, me, Jenny, Jamie and The Moan crawled out into the fresh air.

But fresh air wasn't the only thing waiting for us outside. There was a boy there too. A boy none of us recognized. He had hair so blond it almost looked white, and his eyebrows and eyelashes were the same weird pale colour.

'Hello,' he said, in a weedy, friendly voice.

'Hi,' we all said together, because we're not one of those gangs that attack on sight like a pack of rabid wolves.

'I saw who did it,' the new boy said.

I stepped forward. I was Gang Leader so I was in charge of important discussions.

'Did what?'

'Messed with your den.'

'You mean weed in it?'

'Yes. It was that big boy, the one called Docherty — something like that.'

'Docherty? You mean Dockery?'

'That's it. I've only just moved here so I don't know everyone's name yet. But not just him — his friends were there too.'

Of course.

The Dockery Gang.

The Dockery Gang were the mortal enemies of the Bare Bum Gang. Maybe I should explain why we were called the Bare Bum Gang, which is, I admit, a pretty embarrassing name for a cool gang like us to have. But even explaining how we got the name is quite embarrassing, so all I'll do is say that it began as an insult, but then became something we were proud of, a bit like in the Olden Days, when warriors would show their scars and stumps and things to prove how brave they were.

Back to the wee. There was definitely only one person in the world nasty enough to wee in our den. Some other people might have weed on the roof, but only a criminal mastermind like Dockery would crawl in and wee on the carpet.

And I knew why he'd done it. Dockery and his mob had always wanted to take over our brilliant gang den, which everyone admits is probably the best gang den anywhere in the universe. But even though Dockery and his mates were bigger than us, we'd always managed to thwart – which means stop – their evil plans.

Like all brutal dictators and rotten bullies,

Dockery hated anything good that didn't belong to him. So even though he couldn't capture our den, he wanted to spoil it for us.

And this is what he'd stooped to – weeing in our den, so that it smelled all horrible. He'd probably got his whole gang to save up their wee for hours beforehand so that they had enough of it to ruin our den.

'Are you sure it was him?'

'Pretty sure – big, strong, ugly—'

'That's him all right.'

'What are you going to do about it?'

'Do about it? Mmmm . . . not sure yet. We'll have to think it over. By the way, what's your name?'

'Alfie.'

'Well, Alfie, thank you very much for telling us about Dockery. Sometimes we let new people into our gang. Jennifer, for instance.' I pointed at Jenny, so Alfie would know which one I meant. 'So there's always a chance we might let you in our gang.'

'There's not enough room,' hissed The Moan. 'Not unless someone leaves.'

'Oh yes. But you never know what might happen. One of us might move away or fall into a coma or get attacked by a python—'

'Or a boa constrictor,' said Noah.

'*Or a boa constrictor,*' I continued. 'So you might get a chance. Anyway, you should probably go home now so we can plan our revenge.'

'All right. Bye then,' said Alfie, and he walked off, looking a bit sad.

'I think you should have been nicer to him,' said Noah.

'He did tell us about Dockery,' added Jenny.

'Perhaps you're right,' I said. 'We'll let him play with us next time. But now let's try to shift this stink.'

We threw out the old carpet. That got rid of the worst of the smell, but you could still get a faint whiff of something yucky. Noah went home and came back with some of his mum's incense sticks, and we used our special gang matches to burn them. That took away the last of the wee smell, but The Moan thought the perfumy smell it left instead was even worse.

Luckily our sweet stash hadn't been damaged by the weeing incident. It was in a biscuit tin buried in a hole in the floor, so it would have taken some quite impressive, armour-piercing wee to destroy it, and there's no such thing as that kind of wee.

Chapter Three

THE SPECIAL MIXTURES

So you can see why we all wanted revenge. We had a big debate about what to do. Jamie and The Moan wanted to sneak into the Dockery den and wee all over it.

'We've got to fight wee with wee!' Jamie demanded.

I could see how that would have been fair, but also disgusting.

'We are a civilized gang,' I said. 'We do not go around weeing in other gangs' dens, even if they deserve it.'

'Well what can we do then?' said The

Moan. 'We can't let them get away with it.'

'Science,' I replied. 'Dockery is no better than a baboon, or a pig. He may think it's OK to wee on people's things, but I don't. We're going to invent something better than wee.'

'What do you mean "better than wee"?'

'I mean something even better than wee for making dens smell horrid.'

'Poo?' asked Jamie hopefully.

'No, not poo,' I said wearily. 'Poo is even more disgusting than wee, and not scientific at all. We're going to invent a stinky potion, and attack the Dockery den with that.'

'Brilliant idea,' said Noah, who nearly always supported my plans.

So then we spent the next week developing the right formula. To begin with we tried following the instructions in *George's Marvellous Medicine*, which is an excellent book by Roald Dahl. That meant getting every kind of gloopy stuff from the bathroom and kitchen and garage and mixing them up together. The trouble with that plan was that, even though it looked foul, it ended up smelling quite nice. We didn't try drinking any because then we'd either grow enormous like in the book or, more likely, die in agony of poison.

That was Special Mixture Number One.

Special Mixture Number Two involved us all collecting ear wax, bogeys, sweat and anything else not very nice that came out of our bodies, except for wee and poo (because we're not baboons or savages).

Special Mixture Number Two was a failure because even after a week we only had about a teaspoonful altogether. Noah calculated that to get enough to ruin the Dockery den would take twelve years, by which time we'd all be grown up and have jobs, such as postman (or lady), window cleaner, banker, shop assistant, astronaut, lawyer, doctor (or lady doctor), etc., etc., etc., and we would be too busy to use it.

Special Mixture Number Three was some milk I'd left to go sour, mixed up with an egg I'd left to go bad. It was in my milkshake beaker, because it had a lid. The mixture was coming along quite nicely when my dad found it and drank it, thinking it was a milkshake. He spent the rest of the day in the toilet while Special Mixture Number Three tried to escape out of both ends of him at the same time.

Special Mixture Number Four was made of Marmite mixed with water. I thought it smelled disgusting; so did Noah, but Jennifer and The Moan actually liked it; and Jamie, who would have got the deciding vote, had a blocked nose and so couldn't smell it at all.

Special Mixture Number Five wasn't really a special mixture at all. Jamie had the idea of setting off a whole load of Smarties-tube Fart Bombs (STFBs) inside the enemy den. To begin with we all thought that was quite a good idea, which was a surprise because Jamie had only ever had one good idea in all the time we'd known him. But then Noah worked out that we'd need about a hundred STFBs to properly stink out the den, and the only way to set them off would be by stamping on them actually inside the den. So whoever did the stamping would be caught in the stink blast, and probably stinked (or stunk) to death.

Special Mixture Number Six was good. There was a duck pond in the park on the other side of the town. The water in it was a greeny-browny-slimy-stinky mess. Sometimes you'd see tadpoles wriggling about in the murk, but they always died before they became frogs because the water was so toxic. I think the main reason it was so rank was because the ducks used it as their toilet. We scooped up a bucketful of the water,

making sure we got some of the dead-tadpole-and-duck-poo muck from the bottom of the pond. I mixed it up with a stick. Already it smelled like a tramp's underpants.

'If we leave this to stew for a couple of days, it'll be perfect,' I said.

I kept it in our garage. Every chance I got I went in to check on it. Each day the smell got a little bit worse, but I was still dissatisfied. I never once felt like being sick when I smelled it. It lacked something. So, on the third day, I did a wee in the bucket. That was all it took. The addition of wee turned Special Mixture Number Six into Special Mixture Number Seven.

And, OK, you might say that weeing in the bucket was cheating, after I'd said that weeing was for baboons and pigs, etc., etc. However, I would argue that it was all perfectly scientific, because we had other things in the bucket as well, and mixing stuff up together and seeing how it smells is how science got invented in the first place.

Now all we needed was a Special Mixture Number Seven delivery system. Our combined brains came up with the idea of filling balloons with the mixture, which we would then hurl into the enemy den. One advantage of this plan was that we could use it even if Dockery and his gang were in their den. In fact it would be even better if they were.

So that was why we were marching through the Valley of Doom equipped with the lemonade bottle full of Special Mixture Number Seven, some empty balloons and the funnel to fill them.

Chapter Four

AMBUSHED!

Our den is at one end of the wood, and the Dockery den is at the other. The Dockery den isn't really a proper den at all, but a tent, which is cheating. To reach it we could either have gone round the wood or taken the muddy track that runs through the trees.

After we left the den (I was the last one out to make sure we hadn't left any sweets or anything lying around to attract wild animals, savage beasts, dangerous cannibals, etc., etc.), we decided to take the forest track, because it's more exciting and this was a secret mission after all. The track was probably first made by dinosaurs in the Olden Days when the wood was first invented, and then kept open by sabre-toothed tigers, woolly mammoths, cavemen and knights as time went on.

It always feels like an adventure when you walk through the woods, even though it's not that far from the centre of our town. As soon as you get into the trees, the whole outside world disappears and it's just you and crowding branches, thick ferns, birds and whatever else is lurking in there.

The worst part of the path is called the Valley of Doom. The track follows a brown, scummy stream, always buzzing with gnats and flies. For some reason my dad always calls the stream the Great Grey-Green Greasy Limpopo River, so I usually do too. One minute you're walking along quite happily with the sunlight filtering through the leaves, and the next minute there are steep muddy walls on either side of you and the trees have closed in over your head so it's dark even in the middle of the day. The birds stop singing in the Valley of Doom because it's such a horrible place.

I don't suppose there really are giant blood-sucking leeches in the Valley of Doom, but if they were to live anywhere in the world, then it would definitely be here.

The Valley of Doom took us right behind the enemy camp. It meant that we could sneak up to it without leaving the trees.

It had begun to rain when we set off. Not pouring, but just the sort of steady drizzle you usually get when you plan a picnic. We were walking in single file.

Jennifer was at the front. When you're on a mission in the army, the person at the front is called the 'Point Man', even if they're a girl, like Jennifer. They are probably called 'Point Man' because their job is to point at things – for example enemies that are about to attack you, or nasty patches of nettles that you have to walk around. Being Point Man is the most dangerous job, because you're usually the first one to get blown up (or stung by nettles).

I was next in line, then The Moan, then Noah. Jamie was at the back. The person at the back is always called 'Tail-End Charlie', whatever their real name is. Tail-End Charlie is the second most dangerous position, because you'll get mashed up if you're sneakily attacked from the rear – say by enemy paratroopers, velociraptors, cannibals, etc., etc.

The mission had been uneventful until we reached the Valley of Doom. No casualties so far. Well, except for when Jamie stepped in some kind of animal poo, and we had a big debate about whether it was fox poo or badger poo. I told them that the difference is that badger poo tastes of burnt almonds, but nobody volunteered to try it. Jamie was always unlucky with poo, and if there was any about, he'd be the one to step in it.

Apart from that, the patrol was going to plan. We were excited and a little nervous.

Then we reached the Valley of Doom. The rain got heavier, and it was so gloomy I had to peer to see Jenny a few steps ahead of me. Our line began to bunch together as the Point Man and Tail-End Charlie clustered in towards the rest of us. It was a classic error.

'Spread out,' I said in an urgent whisper. I knew that bunching up made us an easy target for velociraptors, etc.

Then Jenny put up her arm. That was the signal for 'Stop'. We had some other signals too. An arm stretched out to the side meant 'Look over that way'. A finger pointing upwards meant 'Danger, air attack' – for example from dive-bombers or eagles. And a high-pitched girlie scream meant 'Help, I've fallen in quicksand'. Luckily we hadn't had to use any of those yet.

'What is it, Jenny?' I whispered.

'I'm not sure,' she said. 'But I sense there's something wrong.'

'It's quiet,' I said.

'Too quiet,' she replied.

We all knew that was bad news. But it was too late to go back.

'The enemy den is just over there,' I said. 'Five minutes – that's all it'll take.'

Jenny nodded, and we moved on.

If only I'd listened to her.

The first we knew of the attack was when a huge hunk of mud landed in front of Jenny, splattering her nice clean jeans. For a second we didn't realize what was happening. Then more mud began to rain down around us, and we heard a horrible, unearthly war cry – a sound like the yelping of hyenas around a dying wildebeest. It was the jabbering racket that alien invaders would make just as they destroyed the last Earth city.

Dockery and his gang.

'Get the sissies!' they screamed, and worse things — if you can imagine them.

I looked up at the steep muddy sides of the valley. They were like the ramparts of a castle, a castle that completely surrounded us.

'Where are they?' I yelled.

'They're everywhere,' wailed Noah.

You can guess what *he* was on the brink of.

I reached for the binoculars in the case hanging around my neck. Everything was blurred. I fiddled with the focus, and then I saw them. Dark shapes at the top of the muddy slopes. I zoomed in, up to maximum power. It was Dockery, along with the others — William Stanton, James Furbank, Paul Larkin, Carl Hughes. All of them were bigger than us, plus a lot meaner.

If you had a scale of meanness, with Jesus at 1 and Attila the Hun at 10, then the Dockery Gang would be a 9. Maybe even a 9 1/2. That's how bad they were.

They were lobbing huge clods of mud and earth down on us.

The Moan tried to escape by running up one of the slippery mud walls of the valley. He got about halfway up, but then slithered back down.

There was no way out.

I hurled my cheese sandwich up towards the attackers, but it just flapped away like a dying seagull and flopped uselessly down onto the wet earth.

Jennifer rushed to my side. 'What shall we do?'

I was the Gang Leader. I had to decide. I looked all around. They were in front of us and behind us. We were cut off. There was no escape.

'I . . . I . . .'

'Quick, Ludo, you have to tell us what to do. It's your job.'

Now they were all looking at me. Jamie, his honest but not very bright face expecting me to come up with a brilliant plan. The

Moan, waiting for me to mess up so he could moan about it. Noah, my oldest and best friend, ever faithful. Jenny, so brave and so sporty. There had to be something . . .

'Load the bombs,' I said.

'Under combat conditions?' said The Moan. 'But that's impossible!'

'Just do it. Remember your training. Exactly as we planned.'

And for the next two minutes I was incredibly proud of the Bare Bum Gang. Despite the deadly rain of mud and earth landing all around us, we prepared our counter-attack.

The Moan held the balloon, Jenny held the funnel, I poured in the Special Mixture Number Seven, and the first stinky balloon bomb was soon ready. The Moan passed it to Jamie. Jamie may not have been as brainy as Stephen Hawking, but he could throw like a champion. He sent the balloon bomb flying high towards a couple of the enemy gang. It detonated above them in the branches of a tree and sent a shower of Special Mixture Number Seven cascading down on them.

We all cheered.

'Keep going,' I said, and we made the next bomb. Again Jamie sent it flying, this time straight at Dockery. It hit him right on his fat belly and burst, covering him in the stinky green slime.

'One more,' I yelled, 'then we run for it.'

I began to pour Special Mixture Number Seven into the funnel, but then disaster struck. One of the Dockery Gang managed a lucky shot. A mud ball landed right on the funnel as I was pouring. The whole thing seemed to explode, sending Special Mixture Number Seven splashing over all of us. It was in our hair and eyes and mouths and everywhere. It was like falling into the school toilet when it's been blocked for a week. We fell back on the floor, moaning and groaning, defenceless.

Then I heard Dockery yell, 'Charge!' I looked up and saw them coming down the muddy slopes towards us. This was it. We were about to be massacred.

The Bare Bum Gang was going to be utterly, completely, totally wiped out.

Chapter Five

RESCUE?

'Here! This way, quick!'

The voice was familiar, but it took me a few seconds to remember where I'd heard it before.

I looked around.

Nothing.

I tried with the binoculars. The first thing I saw was a rope, trailing down from the valley wall, snaking over the steep, slippery sides towards us. Looking up, I saw a flash of white hair.

It was the new kid. What was his name?

Alfie, that was it. He'd tied the top of the rope round a tree to hold it secure.

Jenny was the first one to react. 'Come on, everyone, get up.'

She dragged Noah and Jamie to their feet. Dockery was coming, half running, half sliding down towards us from the other direction.

That was all we needed to get us going. With Jenny in the lead, we hauled ourselves up the rope, while our feet scrambled on the wet mud of the valley side. There were knots in the rope to help us climb, but it was hard work. In a few seconds Jenny made it. Then, gasping with the effort, I was near the top. The last metre was the hardest, slippery and steep. My hands were burning and sweat was stinging my eyes.

'Give me your stuff,' said Alfie, offering his hand. I gave him my pack and the binoculars in their case.

The Moan and Jamie were right behind me, and soon we were all panting on the wet grass at the top.

Only Noah was still on the rope. He wasn't very strong and he was famously rubbish at climbing. In fact if you listed all his favourite things in the world to do, climbing up a steep slippery bank using a knotted rope with a load of dangerous enemies right behind him would come well down, probably about number 7834, right after being beaten about the face and neck with a large fish.

I went back, leaned over the edge of the bank and stretched down, trying to reach his arm. It was too far. His eyes, filled with fear and pain, looked up into mine, begging me to do something.

Dockery, bellowing like a bull, began to climb the rope. Noah felt the tug, and made a tragic whimpering noise. It was like Jack and the Beanstalk, but in reverse with the ogre chasing Jack up, not down. I felt useless.

Then Alfie, who was taller than me, pushed me out of the way, reached down and hauled Noah to the top.

Dockery was halfway up the rope. He looked up, probably expecting to see me ahead of him. He wore a puzzled expression for a moment when he saw the strange, white-haired figure standing there. That look turned first to rage and then to fear as Alfie took out a penknife and with two quick slashes cut through the rope.

With his fat hands still clutching the useless rope, Dockery slithered down. He landed with a splat right on top of the rest of his gang, who were clustered at the bottom.

It was a truly great moment, but we were too tired to laugh. Not just tired in our bodies, but in our heads as well. It had been such a close-run thing. We were seconds away from utter destruction. Who knows what horrors Dockery and his heavies would have performed?

Chapter Six

THE DISCOVERY

'Everyone OK?' I asked.

'No thanks to you,' moaned The Moan.

'What do you mean?'

'I mean that you led us into a trap, and we could have been wiped out. I don't know what we'd have done without Alfie.'

There was a general murmur of agreement from the rest of the Gang, even Noah.

'And we stink,' said Jamie.

That was true. Special Mixture Number Seven was certainly a glorious success. We stank like something you'd find coming out of an elephant's bum. But no one said how clever I was for inventing it.

'We should get out of here,' said Alfie. 'I mean, before that lot get their act together.'

He pointed down into the valley, where Dockery and his gang were starting to pick themselves up.

'That's for me to decide,' I replied, a bit miffed about all the praise Alfie was getting. The others looked at me in a funny way. 'Right, let's get out of here,' I said.

So we set off back to our den. It was a bit rubbish, because we had to go back through the trees and not along the path. That meant serious nettle trouble. Noah was our Gang Doctor and he always carried lots of dock leaves with him, but soon his supplies were used up. By the time we reached the den we were sore and tired and soaking wet from the rain.

I decided I had to cheer everyone up.

'I think we've earned a visit to the sweet stash.'

'That's the first good idea you've had in about two years,' said The Moan.

'That's not fair,' said Noah. 'Ludo's had lots of good ideas.'

'Name one.'

'Well . . . there was . . . um . . . I can't remember, but I'm sure there must be one.'

All this was going on as we were squeezing through the door of the den.

When we were all in, I saw Alfie's head and shoulders following us.

'Excuse me,' I said. 'What do you think you're doing here? This is our den and you have to get special permission to come in.'

'Oh, sorry, I—'

'Ignore him,' said Jenny. 'Just come on in. You can share our sweets as a thank-you for saving us.' Then she turned to me. 'Actually, Ludo, I'm ashamed of you. We owe Alfie a big thanks, and you've just been rude to him.'

'I haven't been rude! I was going to let him come in, but I wanted him to ask permission first, not just barge in like that.'

'He didn't barge in,' said Jamie. 'He came in in the normal way, crawling like the rest of us.'

'That's not what I— Oh, fine.'

'No, Ludo's right,' said Alfie. 'I should have asked first. Is it OK if I come in?'

'Yes!' they all shouted.

'Everyone happy now?' I asked, still a bit disgruntled. 'Right, let's get the stash.'

We didn't have carpet on the floor any more because of having been weed on by you-know-who. What we had now was newspaper, which wasn't very classy, but better than the raw earth. We had considered putting dried grass on top of the newspaper, but decided against it in case it made us look like rabbits living in a hutch.

Jamie was nearest, so he peeled back the newspaper from over the hole and took out the biscuit tin. Whenever we did this, it was always a very solemn and serious occasion, a bit like going to church, because the sweet stash is the soul of our gang. If we'd been living in the Olden Days we'd probably have worshipped the sweet stash as our god and danced around it wearing special hats.

Plus, of course, eating sweets is about the best thing you can do with your mouth, or probably any part of your body. Not that you can eat sweets with any part of your body except your mouth, although at a pinch you could stuff them up your nose, and I know for a fact that Jamie has tried that a few times.

Jamie put the sweet stash down in the middle of us. There was always a few seconds of silence before I shared the sweets out. I looked around the circle of faces. We'd been through a tough time, but there's nothing so bad that eating sweets won't put it right, except maybe toothache.

Jamie slowly removed the lid.

There followed a completely different kind of silence – the sort of silence that actually sounds louder than bombs.

The tin had been full of every kind of brilliant sweet. Chews, lollies, chocolate, wine gums. You name it and we had it.

Now there was nothing.

No, worse than nothing. There were some stones. Not even cool stones like diamonds, rubies or sapphires. Just plain stony stones.

'Is this some kind of joke, Ludo?' said The Moan, looking at me without smiling. 'Because this isn't a good time to be joking. Have you hidden them? If you have, I think you should get them out. Now. Right now.'

'No . . . I . . . I don't know what's going on.'

Then there was quite a lot of general mayhem. The Gang lost its cool in a big way. They were all shouting at me and looking around the den, in case the sweets had been hidden in some nook or cranny.

I didn't know what to do or think, but

just sat there like a dummy.

After a couple of minutes they all stopped searching, and gathered back around me. It was like the Spanish Inquisition, whatever that is, only worse.

'Ludo,' said Jenny, her face grim, 'do you know what's happened to the sweets?'

'Of course I don't. I'm as puzzled as you.'

'But you were the last person in here before we set off on the mission, weren't you?' said The Moan.

'Well, maybe. I can't remember. But even if I was, I could hardly have scoffed all our stash then, could I? You'd have to be a circus freak to eat that many sweets all in one go.'

'To be honest,' said The Moan, 'I don't know what you're capable of. For all we know you might have a part-time job in the circus eating sweets.'

'Do they need anyone else?' asked Jamie hopefully.

Everyone ignored him.

'Do you promise,' said Noah, I think trying to be helpful, 'that you haven't stolen our sweets?'

'Of course I haven't. I've never . . .' But then I paused, and that pause was fatal.

You see, I couldn't promise that I'd never, ever had the odd extra sweet out of the stash. Being Gang Leader, I did more work than the others, especially high-grade thinking work, such as coming up with new plans, traps, etc., etc., etc., so I sometimes needed extra energy – for example from sweets. Plus I put the most sweets into the stash in the first place, especially ones I don't like, such as coconut-flavoured Quality Street.

But that pause after 'never' made them all point at me, and say things like: 'See, see, he did it, it was him.'

I tried saying no, but I was drowned out. I felt weak and helpless and I wanted to cry, but I didn't because I'm brave. Instead of crying I hung my head.

After a minute Noah said, 'Ludo, do you absolutely swear on the Holy Bible that you never took any sweets out of the stash?'

'That's not fair,' I began, 'I . . .'

And I was going to explain about the odd sweet I'd taken in the past, and after that I'd swear on any bible from any religion in the world they liked, including Hindu, Buddhist, Eskimo, Inca, etc. etc., that it wasn't me that had scoffed the whole stash this time, when Jenny's clear voice rang out.

'What's this?'

The Gang swivelled towards her. She was holding up my binocular case. There was something different about it. A tiny corner of shiny gold paper was poking out from under the flap of

the case. Jenny popped it open. The case was crammed full of sweet wrappers. In fact it was so full they literally burst out like a firework display, all gold and green and red and silver and blue.

I think I'd have been happier then if they'd all gone crazy. But what happened was worse, much worse. It was a sort of groan, long and sad and desolate. The sound you sometimes hear on an animal programme when a baby whatever – say zebra or whale – loses its mother.

It was the sound of friendship dying.

'Oh, Ludo,' said Noah, on the brink of, well, you know. 'How could you?'

'But . . . but . . . but . . .'

The truth was I was as stunned as any of them.

Chapter Seven

THE TRAGIC FALL
OF LUDO

'Maybe it was an accident or something,'
said Alfie softly. 'Or maybe Ludo ate the
sweets and then just, well, forgot about it.'

I looked at him. His face was completely
blank, and it was impossible to know what
was going on in his head.

'Anyway,' he continued, 'it was my
birthday a week ago, and I've still got some
birthday money left over. I can buy you all
some new sweets.'

'That's very good of you,' said Jenny, her
face as stern as a statue. I mean as stern

as a stern statue. You probably get smiling statues, but she was way sterner than that.

'I've heard enough,' said The Moan, as if he was in charge. 'Outside, everyone.'

Almost without knowing how, I found that I was standing outside the den. All my old friends were in a line facing me, with Alfie sitting on a tree stump over to one side.

The Moan was talking.

'When you started out as Gang Leader, I thought you were all right at it. Not brilliant, but not too rubbish. But now you've led us into a fiasco in the Valley of Doom, and we got all stunk up and, what's more, you've eaten all our sweets. That makes you a thief, as well as an idiot and a loser. If you had just been an idiot, or just a thief, or just a loser, then we might have let you stay in the Gang. But as you're all three, we've got to kick you out.' He looked at the others. 'All agreed?'

Noah had tears welling up in his eyes, but he said nothing. Jenny looked sad and

47

serious, and said, 'Agreed,' in a quiet voice.

Jamie said, 'Agreed,' in a loud voice, at the same time as scratching his bottom and picking his nose.

No one spoke up for me.

'And as there's now room in the den for another person, I say we let Alfie in to take Ludo's place. Everyone agree to that too?'

There was a general 'yes' sound.

'Have you anything to say before we pass sentence?'

'I think you've already passed sentence,' whispered Jenny.

'Oh yes. Well, have you anything to say before we, er, carry out the sentence.'

He made it sound like I was about to go to the guillotine, which is how the French used to chop people's heads off before they invented the firing squad to kill people.

I took a moment to steady myself. It's important to have Famous Last Words. It's one of the things you'll be remembered for, such as Julius Caesar's '*Et tu Brute*', which he said after he'd been nastily stabbed in the togas, and Oscar Wilde saying, '*Either the wallpaper goes or I do.*'

'Yes, I have. I didn't steal those sweets. I know it looks bad, with the wrappers being in my binocular case and everything, but I just didn't, and if you were ever truly my friends then you'd believe me. And I think we did quite well in the Valley of Doom, considering we were ambushed. Some people might say it was our finest hour. Anyway, I invented this gang and it wouldn't exist without me, but I don't want to be in any gang that doesn't want me in it. So it's goodbye. You'll never see me again.'

'Except at school,' said Noah.

'Yes, well, of course we'll see each other at school. It'd be hard not too.'

'And at Scouts,' said Jamie.

'Yes, I suppose I'll see you at Scouts too, sometimes.'

'And generally around the place, like at

the shops,' said The Moan. 'But we'll ignore you.'

'I'll ignore you even more,' I replied.

And then, without another word or turning back, I left them for ever.

Probably.

Chapter Eight

POOR OBI-WAN

'You can't stay in there all day, Ludo.'

That showed what my mum knew. I was going to stay in my bedroom all day and nobody could stop me. She was shouting because I'd piled everything in my bedroom up behind the door to jam it so she couldn't get in.

This is what I crammed behind the door:

- my gigantic box of Lego (just the ordinary bits, not my Star Wars Lego, which is way too precious);

- my jaguar (or maybe leopard) pyjama case stuffed with all my old dressing-up clothes;
- all the books from my bookcase;
- my remote-controlled truck that hadn't had any batteries since I was four;
- my shoes (trainers, ordinary school shoes and Sunday best);
- my box of interesting stones (including the priceless Sea Emerald my dad found for me on the beach in Devon);
- my pillows;
- my duvet;
- my underpants;
- my real working microscope that I'd never actually managed to see anything through at all, despite trying with hair, flies, blood, bogeys and drops of water out of the toilet that should have been squirming with interesting germs.

So, as you see, it would take more than just one mum to bash her way in. Unless she was

driving a bulldozer, or had a bazooka.

'It's your favourite dinner.'

I was actually quite hungry, because of not having any sweets after the mission. But no matter how hungry I was, I wouldn't open the door because I didn't want my mum and dad and my sister Ivy to see my eyes. If they did, they might think that I'd been crying, even though I hadn't.

My eyes were red and watery because I had something in them. Probably a fly. Yes, that was it. Two flies had flown into my eyes. Or maybe one fly had flown into both of them. Not at the same time, because then it would have to be the size of a pigeon or giant bat or something, and it wouldn't have been happy with just making my eyes water but would have tried to suck out all of my blood too. No, it was just a standard fly, and it must have flown into one eye and then escaped, but had been so confused it then flew into the other eye. Yes, that was definitely it.

'It's fish and chips.'

Fish and chips. I love fish and chips. I eat the chips first, and then the inside of the fish, and then the crinkly batter last – I like the crinkly batter best. The only bad thing about it was having to watch Ivy eat mushy peas, which was like watching a zombie suck the brains out of its victim.

My stomach made a loud growling noise

like a black panther announcing his lordship over all the beasts of the jungle. And if you think that the lion is the Lord of the Jungle, then you're wrong, because lions don't even live in the jungle, but where it's all grassy. And if you think Tarzan is the Lord of the Jungle, then you're just plain silly, because he's only a story.

'I'm not eating any mushy peas.'

'I know you're not.'

'And you can't try to persuade me to, even by bribing me.'

'Whatever you like. Just come down. I know you're upset.'

'I'M NOT UPSET!'

'Whatever you say.'

'I'll think about it.'

It took me a few minutes to clear the mess from the door. Mum and Dad looked at each other when they saw me. Ivy had a gigantic chip in her fist, holding it as if it was a spear. Good idea, that, I thought. I mean, an edible spear. For example, if you were out hunting in the jungle and got lost, you could eat it. Not that a chip would be much use if you got attacked by cannibals. They'd just eat you and then have the chip as a side order.

After I'd finished my fish and chips (plus some of Ivy's that she didn't want and hadn't dribbled any mushy pea juice over) I went back to my bedroom. Then Dad came up for a chat. It was obviously his turn.

'What's up, son?' he asked in the special voice he always used when he wanted to sound like he cared about my problems.

'Nothing.'

'Is it your elasticated trousers? That's what your mother thinks.'

My mum had bought me a pair of trousers with a stretchy elastic waist. Some of the other kids made fun of them because they were babyish. They said they were stretchy so I could fit a nappy inside them. I'd forgotten how much I hated my elasticated trousers, but now Dad

had reminded me.
That made me
even more sad.

'No.'

'Is it your hair?'

Mum had cut
my hair at the
weekend. It looked
like a vulture had
landed on my head
and died. That was
another thing to be
depressed about.

'No.'

'Is it because Ivy ate Obi-Wan?'

'IVY DID WHAT?'

My Lego Obi-Wan Kenobi character was one of my favourite things in the world, and now my sister had eaten him. Now there was no one to fly the Jedi Interceptor. Just how bad were things going to get?

'Oh, sorry, didn't you know? Don't worry, we'll get him when he comes out the other end. We'll wash all the you-know-what off. He'll be good as new.'

This was turning into the worst cheering-up session in the history of the world. I decided that I'd better tell Dad why I was sad before he made things even worse by telling me that the universe was about to end, or that Granny and Grandad were coming to stay.

'I got chucked out of the Gang, Dad.'

And then, because I'd said it, straight out like that, I did cry, but only a little bit. Dad gave me a hug, and I told him the whole story, except the part about doing a wee in the Special Mixture Number Seven.

'Never mind,' he said. 'You'll soon make some new friends.'

'How can I? There isn't anyone else to play with.'

'What about Jules and Jim?'

Jules and Jim were two manky twins. They were five years old and the only game they could play was pulling hair. You'd have to do a lot of thinking before you came up with a game as rubbish as pulling hair.

'I'd rather eat my own ear in a sandwich.'

'Oh . . . Well, would you like me to have a word with Noah's dad? Noah's your best friend, isn't he?'

'Definitely not. It's Noah I hate the most now. He should have stuck up for me.'

'OK then, Ludo, why don't you sleep on it tonight, and we'll have a think about what to do in the morning? Things always look better in the morning.'

'You don't.'

'What?'

'You always look terrible in the morning, like someone's come and beaten you up in the night.'

'Ha ha,' said Dad, and ruffled my hair. He was quite a good dad, really.

I read my comics late into the night. It seemed that every superhero had a helper or a friend or a gang. I was the only one who was completely alone, unless you included my Obi-Wan, all covered in Ivy poo.

And it was somewhere in that long, lonely night that I began to *Think the Unthinkable*.

Chapter Nine

ALFIE

So I thought *The Unthinkable*, but before I actually had to do *The Unthinkable* (or do I mean *The Undoable*?), I decided to have a little chat with the person who had brought me to this terrible situation.

I'd noticed that Alfie always got to school early so he could suck up to the teachers without any of the kids noticing. That's the kind of squirt he was. So the next day, I got up half an hour before normal, and ran all the way to school so I could catch him. I hid behind the school gates, peeping out through one of the gaps in the wood.

Alfie got dropped off in a car by his mum. She gave him a big wet kiss on the cheek, the kind you could hear going off like a depth charge in a submarine film. *Whuuuuump!* it went. Then she wiped the red lipstick stain off with her hanky while he squirmed and looked around in case anyone had seen.

Well, I had.

As soon as he came through the gates I jumped out in front of him. He looked surprised for about a second. Then he said, quite calmly, as if we were old chums, 'Hello, Ludo.'

That took me by surprise, which was the opposite of what was supposed to be happening (i.e. me taking *him* by surprise).

'Hello,' I said.

'Nice to see you.'

'Yes. Nice to see you too,' I replied.

And then I remembered what I was there for.

'No, actually it isn't nice to see you. In fact, seeing you is completely rubbish. I'd rather see a giant pile of steaming monkey poo served up on my plate for dinner.'

'Really? Then why were you waiting for me? You must really like monkey poo for dinner. I'll have to tell the others later.'

You had to admit, this Alfie was a cool customer. Well, two could play at that game. I mean, the game of being a cool customer.

'Exactly,' I replied. 'I rest my case.'

'Exactly what?' said Alfie, looking a bit puzzled, as well he might.

'You admit that you'd rather eat sweets than monkey poo?'

'Yes, of course . . . Who wouldn't, except a loony like you.'

'So then, you admit it was you who ate our gang sweets?'

'Ah, so that's what this is all about. Look, Ludo, why don't you just let it go? The Bare Bum Gang doesn't want you, doesn't *need* you. We've moved on – why don't you? Get a life. Make some new friends. Find a new hobby. Whittle a stick. Collect some stamps.'

'I know exactly what you did,' I said, beginning to lose my temper. 'You made some kind of a sneaky plan with Dockery. You knew we were going to get ambushed, and that's why you were right there to rescue us. And you'd already scoffed our sweets and hidden them in my binocular case . . .'

I sort of dwindled into silence then, because I didn't have any proof of what I'd said and I could see from the smile on Alfie's face that he knew it.

'It doesn't matter what you think,' he said, still smiling. 'Everyone knows you're a liar and a sweet-stealer and a useless Gang Leader. They all like me more than you.' And then he paused and his face suddenly looked so sly you could have used it to show what the word 'sly' meant to someone who was learning how to speak English – say an alien or a Frenchman. 'Especially Jenny,' he continued. 'She told me how much more she likes me than you.'

Well, that was too much for me.

'You keep your horrible slimy hands off her, you monster,' I yelled.

And I admit, I seriously considered giving him a jolly good thump on the side of the head. But I didn't, because even thoughhe was a bit taller than me, he was weakand skinny, so it would be bullying. Anyway, it would be descending to his level and you shouldn't use violence to solve arguments, unless you're arguingwith the Nazis, and violence is the only language they understand. Except German, of course.

So I gave him a little poke on the shoulder instead. And when I say a little poke, I don't really mean a gigantic big poke. I mean a really, really little poke. Hard enough to, say, knock a ladybird off a twig or burst a spit bubble, but not hard enough to poke through a piece of tissue paper. Unless you'd just blown your nose on it, and you had a really runny cold. So what I'm saying is I didn't poke him very hard at all.

But the way he acted you'd have thought I'd shot him with a high-powered rifle. And not in the shoulder, but right in the middle of his eye. He threw himself down and writhed around in agony, holding his face.

'My eye! My eye!' he screamed. 'I'm blinded. Blinded for life.'

It was then that I heard the gasp behind me. I spun round to see the whole of the Bare Bum Gang there, along with a load of other children just arriving for school. Alfie had seen them coming, and that was why he went into his act. It was obvious. They must have realized what he was up to. Mustn't they?

'That is just about the nastiest thing I've ever seen,' said Jenny.

'Yeah, I know,' I began. 'I mean, the way he—'

But Jenny shoved me aside as easily as you throw the duvet off your bed in the morning.

'Poking a kid in the eye,' said The Moan, following close behind Jennifer, 'is the worst thing you can do. It's not fighting fair. It's cheating. Everyone knows that.'

'But I didn't . . . I . . . it was . . .'

But it was all too late. They crowded around Alfie and no one was listening to me.

'He just poked me in the eye for no reason,' said Alfie, from the middle of the crowd.

'Do you want me to bash him?' said Jamie.

'No,' said Alfie. 'Just leave him. He isn't worth it.'

'You're right,' said Jenny. 'He isn't.'

All I could see was their backs closed against me. I was alone.

OK, I thought. That's it.

Time to do *The Unthinkable*.

Or *The Undoable*.

Or whatever it was.

Chapter Ten

THE UNTHINKABLE (OR THE UNDOABLE)

'You? What do you want?'

That huge ugly head with the eyes, nose and mouth all squished together in the middle of his face peered out at me from the flap at the front of the Dockery Gang tent.

I swallowed hard and said it.

'I want to be in your gang.'

Dockery, followed by Stanton, Furbank, Larkin and Hughes, piled out of the tent. It hadn't looked big enough to hold them all, but somehow they'd all squeezed in, and now they squeezed out.

They formed a circle all around me.

'Is this some kind of a joke?' said Dockery. 'Because if it is, it isn't funny.'

'It's not a joke. I'm not in the Bare Bum Gang any more. I want to be in your gang.'

Now, you're probably amazed and disgusted by this. I know I would be, if I were you. How could I even dream of joining the evil Dockery Gang? Weren't they all bullies and wicked villains and really, really naughty?

Yes.

Yes.

And yes.

But I had no gang and no friends. I was alone and defenceless in a cruel world. I thought that even a rubbish, nasty gang like Dockery's was better than no gang at all. And there was something else. I wanted to prove to the Bare Bum Gang that I didn't need them, that I could do perfectly well without them, thank you very much.

Dockery smiled. It wasn't pretty. He looked like a turnip that'd been hit with a spade. Then he laughed. It sounded like the screeching of a baboon with rabies. As he laughed the rest of his gang joined in.

Then Dockery gave me a shove. One of the others had knelt down behind me so I tripped over him and fell on my back. The oldest trick in the book, but I had fallen for it. Now they all laughed so hard I thought they were going to throw up.

'Why should we let you into our gang?' said Dockery when he'd calmed down.

'I know where the Bare Bum Gang keep their sweets. And I know where all the traps are.'

I was still lying on my back. I hadn't been able to get up because Dockery had his fat foot on my chest.

There was a flicker of interest in Dockery's eyes. He had good cause to fear the traps around the Bare Bum Gang den. Many times he'd fallen into one of the Smarties-tube Fart Bomb traps, or a Squirty Ink trap, or even the much-feared Dog Poo trap.

'But I don't get it. Why do you want to be in our gang?' he said slyly. 'You've always been our mortal enemy.'

'I don't want to talk about it. Let's just say I have my reasons.'

Dockery looked deep into my eyes, trying to see if I was lying or not. Obviously he didn't know that I never told lies. Well, not unless I really had to, like in an emergency – say if we were invaded by aliens and I knew where the Prime Minister was hiding, and I told the aliens he was in Peru, rather than in our garden shed, or whatever.

'How do I know this isn't some sort of trick?'

'Because I'm here, and you've got me, and if it was a trick you could marmalize me.'

Marmalizing was something Dockery understood all too well. He gave a little nod, took his foot off my chest and held out his hand to pull me up off the ground. But as this was still Dockery, when I'd got halfway up he let go and I fell back in the mud, which set off the baboon-laughing all over again.

Then they trooped back into their tent and I was left alone, not knowing what to do. A few seconds later, Carl's greasy head came poking through the tent flap.

'You coming in or not?' he said with a

smirk. Or was it a scowl? Actually it was in between — a smowl or a scirk.

Whatever it was, I followed him into the dark smelly interior of the Dockery den.

Chapter Eleven

THE TEST

It was pitch black. I was in Mrs Cake's front garden.

I was holding the rotten egg.

Dockery and his gang had a supply of rotten eggs that they kept in their den the same way the Bare Bum Gang kept sweets. Dockery had written dates on them in felt tip. Some of them were two years old, which was how you knew they were really, really rotten. Eggs of Mass Destruction, you could call them.

I sneaked up to the front door. I could hear the snickering Dockery and his greasy friends behind the hedge.

I was supposed to throw the Egg of Mass Destruction through Mrs Cake's letter box. I wasn't happy about this, and I knew it was a Bad Thing, but it was the only way I'd be allowed to join the Gang.

I reached the door. I could see some light escaping from between a chink in the curtains, and I could hear the telly. I paused.

'Get on with it, poo-brain,' hissed Dockery from behind me. 'We haven't got all night.'

With my heart in my throat I carefully lifted up the flap. The sound of the telly spilled out. People were laughing. I held the egg up in front of the opening. I felt sick. I felt dirty.

'Come on,' said Dockery, louder this time.

I put the egg through the letter box.

Except that I didn't.

I tried to, but it wouldn't fit. Tap-tap-tap, it went, as the shell clicked against the metal.

I was so relieved I could have cheered. It was great. I'd tried to post the egg, but it wouldn't fit. I'd done my best, so they'd have to let me in the Gang, but poor old Mrs Cake wouldn't have stinky egg on her floor.

I let the letter-box flap fall shut. It sounded as loud as an explosion. The next thing I heard was Trixie yapping like a demented yapping machine invented by a mad scientist. Trixie was Mrs Cake's Jack Russell terrier. Her favourite food was children's legs. That's Trixie, I mean, not Mrs Cake, who'd probably never even tasted a child's leg.

I don't know why, but somehow the yapping dog froze me. I just couldn't move. It was as if I'd been zapped with a paralysing ray.

The top half of the door was made of knobbly-wobbly glass, and I could see Trixie jumping up on the inside, her pointy snout snarling and snapping. I suppose you shouldn't really be afraid of a dog that's only a little bit bigger than a rat, but Trixie was definitely scary. After all, quite a few things are small and scary – like scorpions, black widow spiders, evil dwarfs and Brussels sprouts.

And then, looming up behind Trixie, I saw the dark shadow of Mrs Cake herself. We used to say that Mrs Cake was a witch, but that was silly, because you don't really get witches any more, except in books. But even though I knew she couldn't be a witch, and that she was, in fact, quite nice, I was still a little bit worried that if she caught me putting a smelly rotten egg through her door she might turn me into a frog, or at least give me warts.

The egg was still in my hand. Mrs Cake fiddled with the latch on her door. I crammed the egg into my back pocket the second before the door opened.

Mrs Cake smiled. Trixie snarled.

'Hello, dear,' she said. Mrs Cake, I mean, not Trixie.

'H-h-h-hello.'

'It's little Ludo, isn't it? What is it you want? Is your football in the back garden again?'

'N-n-n-n-no. Sorry. I, er, came round to see if you needed anything. At school our teacher said we had to ask helpless old people if they wanted us to go shopping for them or rescue them if they were in danger or just be nice to them if they were sad and lonely because they had nothing interesting in their lives apart from *Countdown* and *Coronation Street*.'

That part was actually true, although I can't remember if those were Miss Bridges' actual words. Anyway, I said it all so quickly that I doubt if Mrs Cake understood it all.

'How kind,' she said. 'Why don't you come inside and I'll see if I've got something nice for you?'

No one had ever been inside Mrs Cake's bungalow before. It was obviously a trap. She was going to lure me in so she could wartify me in private.

I expected it to smell of old lady in there, but it just smelled of house. Her carpet, though, was so thick I thought I was going to sink into it up to my neck.

'Just come into the living room and I'll get you some sweets. Or would you rather have a pickled onion?'

'Some sweets, please.'

Then Trixie started to bite my shoes, which made me jump up and down, while Mrs Cake shouted, 'No, Trixie, no!' Finally she wrestled the horrid little dog into the kitchen and then out of the back door.

'You sit down, dear,' she shouted (Mrs

Cake, not Trixie). There was a baggy old chair and a baggy old sofa. I sat on the sofa.

CRUNCH.

STINK.

The egg!

The gloopy slime oozed over my backside and the stench rose up like poison gas.

Mrs Cake came in, smiling, carrying a plate of biscuits.

'Sorry, got to go,' I yelled. 'I've had an accident!' And I ran out of the room and through the hall and out of the front door, trailing the eggy cloud behind me.

If there was an Olympic gold medal for embarrassment, I'd have won it.

Chapter Twelve

YIPPEE!

It was the next evening, a Sunday, and I was standing in front of the Dockery Gang outside their den, explaining what had happened.

'You sat on the rotten egg?' Dockery was laughing so hard that tears rolled down his fat face.

'And you said you'd had an accident, so the old bat probably thought you'd pooed your pants,' added Larkin, a big line of slimy drool dangling out of his mouth.

'It wasn't funny,' I said. 'My mum had

to throw my trousers away because of the smell. They were my third favourite pair.'

The whole lot of them were bent double by now, laughing like hyenas.

'OK, boys,' said Dockery at last. 'I say he's in. I haven't laughed so much since Miss Bridges slipped and broke her arm in the playground last year.'

'I didn't think that was very funny,' I said.

I liked Miss Bridges. She was kind and also good at doing the voices when she read us a story.

'Yeah, well, that shows what you know,' Larkin replied, stepping up close to me. 'Because it was funny. But not as funny as this.' Then he tried to push me in the chest. But this time it didn't work. I'd noticed one of the others had moved behind me, and I knew they were going to do the same trick again. When Larkin shoved, I dodged to one side, and he stumbled forward and fell over Furbank, who was the one kneeling down. They ended up sprawling together on the floor.

I thought I might be in for it from the others, but they laughed even harder than they had when it was me falling over or getting rotten egg on his trousers. Weird sort of gang, I thought, where they're not even nice to each other.

Dockery dragged them both up off the ground and gave them a little shake.

'Enough messing about, boys,' he said, still chuckling. 'We've got to have a little celebration to, er, celebrate our new member.'

'Good idea,' said Larkin. 'Sweets and Coke, that's what we want.'

Dockery loomed over me. 'Right, give us two pounds then,' he said.

'Two pounds!' I exclaimed. 'What do you mean?'

'Three pounds then. It goes up every time you complain.'

'I'm not complaining, I just didn't realize I had to pay to be in.'

'Four pounds. Do you want to be in this gang or not?'

Actually, I wasn't sure any more. I'd decided that there might be worse things in life than not being in a gang, especially if the gang tried to make you be horrible to old ladies and then gave you smelly trousers. But it was hard to say that when Dockery was looming over me like an evil German zeppelin bomber airship.

So I nodded.

'Cough up then,' said Larkin.

'I haven't got any money with me.'

'Well, you'd better go and get some then.'

So I went home, got the four pounds out of my talking robot piggy bank, and brought it back. Then Dockery sent me to the newsagent's to get the supplies. I wasn't allowed to have any of the Coke or sweets because that was the rule.

But it was done.

I was in.

I was officially a member of the Dockery Gang.

Yippee.

Chapter Thirteen

THE SHOE

I was sitting by myself at break time the next day. I was reading my space-dinosaur book, which is one of my favourites. It's about dinosaurs in space. They fight other dinosaurs, who are also in space. It's one of the best books ever written about dinosaurs in space. But for once I couldn't concentrate on it. Jenny, Noah, The Moan and Jamie were chatting together. I wanted to go and talk to them, maybe hang out for a bit. I even closed my book, using a piece of cabbage I'd hidden in my pocket to keep my page. (I'd hidden the cabbage in my pocket because otherwise Mrs Muffit, the dinner lady, would have made me eat it at lunch time.) But then, before I'd had time to get up, Alfie joined them, and he said something. They all looked at me quickly and giggled.

It was because they were laughing at me that they didn't see Dockery and his gang come sneaking up. They had to sneak up these days because of Jenny. Jenny was a black belt at every martial art you've ever heard of, including tae kwon do, karate, bum-kicking and happy slapping, so sneaking up followed by lightning attacks and running away was their only hope. They grabbed hold of Noah, and wrestled him to the ground. Furbank ripped off one of his shoes and chucked it to me before Jenny could do anything to stop them.

I wasn't expecting the shoe, but I caught it anyway, because I'm good at catching as long as it's not something hard like a cricket ball or a Ninja death star.

'Throw it on the roof,' Dockery yelled at me.

There was a flat roof covering the bike shed. It was where things always got thrown – shoes, lunchboxes, Year One kids.

I could feel everyone looking at me. The Dockery Gang, the Bare Bum Gang, the Commandos (that was another gang who weren't our enemies or our friends), even the ordinary no-gang kids.

I sensed that this was a Decisive Moment in World History. What happened next would change my life for ever, along with the lives of everyone else involved and possibly the whole planet, including Alaska and Borneo.

It came down to this:

I could throw the shoe on top of the bike shed or I could give it back to Noah.

I thought for a second.

Then I took very, very careful aim.

And I threw the shoe.

It sailed through the air towards the bike-shed roof. It looked like a perfect shot, but then it dipped, pinged off the gutter and bounced on the ground.

Normally by now Jenny would have been busy chasing off the Dockery Gang, handing out a few slaps and kicks (if you can hand out a kick, that is – I suppose really you have to foot it out). But she ignored the Dockery Gang, and came up to me. Her face was an interesting purple colour. Usually her hair was arranged to look like a volcano exploding out of the top of her head, but today she had it in about four (or maybe five) plaits, all sticking out in different directions. She reminded me of that famous monster from Greek mythology called the Medusa, who has snakes instead of hair, and if you looked at her you turned into stone and then died in horrible agony.

That should probably have been a warning.

'Hello, Jenny,' I said.

Or that's what I tried to say. What I actually said was:

'Hell—OW!' and then I fell, not on the floor, but into a big square plastic box that was behind me. The box was half full

of beanbags, which made it actually quite a nice thing to fall into. The headmistress, Mrs Plunket, had insisted that there was a box of beanbags in the playground, which she thought would provide interesting entertainment for us children. I suppose she honestly believed we'd toss them gently to each other, boys and girls all playing nicely together. Or perhaps we'd practise walking about with them balanced on our heads. She was mistaken in that view.

As I lay in the beanbag box, Jenny came and loomed over me. I knew better than to try to get out. She'd only push me back in again. Also, Jenny was polite and well brought up and didn't hit people when they were cowering on the floor, or in boxes, although I was hardly cowering at all, more just sort of lying there, looking up at the sky and minding my own business.

'I hoped we might have been wrong about you, Ludo,' she said, sounding more sorrowful than angry. 'But now I see we weren't. You're just a dirty Dockery dog. I can't believe I ever liked you even a bit.'

I wanted to explain some things to Jenny. I wanted to explain that I'd have given anything to be back in the Bare Bum Gang. That I didn't want to be in Dockery's stinky gang. That I'd deliberately aimed the shoe so that it bounced off the gutter, and that it was probably the best throw I'd ever done in my life, because any old idiot could have just thrown it up on the roof. I wanted to explain that Jenny was my favourite girl in the whole world, the only one I didn't think was really silly, the only one I liked to sit next to in the Gang den or anywhere else.

But I didn't say any of that. I couldn't think of the words until it was too late and Jenny's back was turned. I could have sworn the snakes hissed and spat at me as she walked away.

Chapter Fourteen

OVERHEARD

So, that wasn't very good, I think you'll agree. I stayed in the box and closed my eyes and kept them shut until the bell sounded. I didn't want to see anything that was happening around me, because it would most likely be something terrible, and the chance of it being anything apart from terrible was maybe one in a million.

It was actually quite pleasant, lying there on top of the soft beanbags as the playground sounds grew quiet, like the water slowly growing cold around you in the bath.

Lying there meant I was going to be late back into class, but I decided I'd tell Miss Bridges that I'd fallen down and hurt myself and that was why I was late, which was nearly true.

I'd just decided to get up when I heard some voices. Quiet voices. Not quiet because they were far away, but quiet because they were whispering. It's always extra interesting when people whisper. In fact whispering is the worst way of keeping a secret, because people always know you're saying something worth listening to. Especially if the whispers are angry whispers.

I peeped over the top of the box

The first thing I saw was Dockery's back. The next thing was Alfie's front. Alfie and Dockery were whispering together. I strained hard to hear

what they were saying:

'You filthy sneak. You betrayed us. You were supposed to betray them. We had them cornered in the woods, and you helped them get out. You get a thump for that.'

'No, no, it was all part of the plan.'

Then there were some bits I could hardly hear at all, except for the odd word: 'Money . . . sweets . . . Ludo . . . Bare Bum . . . ha ha ha.' That sort of thing. And then I saw Alfie give something to Dockery. It looked like it might have been money, although it could also have been an amulet or some magic beans, although that's not very likely.

'I'll let you off, this time,' said Dockery, louder. 'But any more mess-ups and you're gonna find yourself wearing your own bum for a hat.'

Then they both started to walk back towards the classrooms, and I ducked down into the beanbag box.

Interesting.

Very interesting, I thought (I mean about Dockery and Alfie, not the beanbag box, which was really quite boring).

But what could it all mean?

Chapter Fifteen

AN UNEXPECTED VISITOR

The doorbell rang. It was half past seven, and I'd just finished my literacy home-work, which was all to do with words, and I was about to start my numeracy home-work, which was mainly to do with numbers.

When our doorbell rang it was usually someone asking if we wanted to change our gas supplier, or sometimes two nice men asking if we wanted to be saved from the Horrible Burning Fires of Hell. If my dad answered the door, he would either just say no thanks, or sometimes start ranting at them, saying things like, actually he'd rather have his nose chewed off by a pack of weasels.

What I saw when I opened the door surprised me as much as if it had been a pack of nose-eating weasels. Or two packs, for that matter.

Noah.

I have to tell you something about me and Noah, to explain why I was so upset about him not believing me and joining  the others in chucking me out of the Gang. You see, I had known Noah before either of us could even walk. Our mums used to put us in the same playpen together when we were still shuffling about on our bottoms. We used to chew each other's chewy toys, and drink out of the same beaker and even poo in the same potty. When we were three we were sent to the same nursery, a scary place full of children who would bite you given half a chance, and grown-ups who seemed to think that carrot sticks counted as a treat.

At big school we'd stuck together through thick and thin, me watching his back and him watching mine. When we were old enough, we formed the Gang, before it was even called the Bare Bum Gang. I was Leader and he was Gang Doctor. The others, The Moan, Jamie, Jennifer, they all came later. We were the originals. We were the heart. I could stand the others rejecting me, but not Noah.

'Hi,' he said.

'Hi,' I said.

Then we didn't say anything for a few moments. Noah looked at me, and then down at his shoes.

Then he said, 'Can we have a talk?'

'Is it all about what a rubbish leader I was, and how I ate all the sweets, and about how much better things are now that Alfie's in your gang instead of me?'

'No!' said Noah violently. 'It isn't about any of those things.'

And then it all came out in a gush.

'It's terrible now. I hate it. I'm sorry about what we did to you. I know you wouldn't have stolen the sweet stash. Alfie's taken over the Gang and made himself the leader and it's not like it used to be. We don't do anything fun any more, but the others don't really mind because he gives them sweets and presents, especially Jennifer, because he wants her to be his special friend. And none of our traps are properly looked after any more and the Smarties-tube Fart Bombs haven't been filled up for ages, so they probably won't even work if we get attacked. And even worse, Alfie told us that we could do a wee just outside the den, when everyone knows that you have to go at least a hundred metres away when you do a wee or the smell will give away your position to your enemies and wild animals.'

By this stage I'd led Noah into the kitchen and poured him out some milk to calm him down.

'Yes,' I said, in my wise voice, 'it's exactly like the last days of the Roman Empire, when they had rubbish emperors who cared more about feasts and watching ladies dance around with hardly any clothes on than looking after their borders, such as Hadrian's Wall and the Great Wall of China and the Berlin Wall. But what am I supposed to do about it? It's not my gang any more. I'm in the Dockery Gang now.'

'Don't be silly,' he replied. 'I know you're not really in the Dockery Gang. I read about it in a spy book. It's called "being in deep cover". But I saw what you did with my shoe. That's why I came here.

You deliberately threw it so that it hit the gutter, didn't you?'

'Well, er, yes, I suppose . . .'

'And you're only pretending to be in the Dockery Gang, aren't you?'

'Oh, yes, well . . .'

'I knew it. So you're a kind of spy, just finding out their secret plans, aren't you?'

'Yes, that's it, I guess . . .'

And when Noah put it like that, it all fell into place. Yes, I was a secret agent. I did aim the shoe so that it hit the gutter and not the roof. Yes, I was planning a brilliant campaign to defeat our enemies and win back the trust of the Bare Bum Gang.

'Let's go to my room,' I said, 'and I'll tell you all about it.'

The very next day Alfie received a letter written on a scrunched-up piece of paper with bogeys smeared on it. The English was completely rubbish, with useless spelling and bad handwriting, exactly as if the person who wrote it was a stupid big bully. This is what it said:

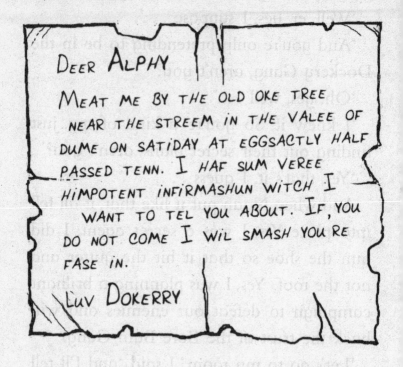

DEER ALPHY

MEAT ME BY THE OLD OKE TREE NEAR THE STREEM IN THE VALEE OF DUME ON SATIDAY AT EGGSACTLY HALF PASSED TENN. I HAF SUM VEREE HIMPOTENT INFIRMASHUN WITCH I WANT TO TEL YOU ABOUT. IF, YOU DO NOT COME I WIL SMASH YOU'RE FASE IN.

LUV DOKERRY

At the same time Dockery received a letter written on pink notepaper decorated with flowers and smelling of perfume. The writing was incredibly neat and the spelling was perfect. In fact just the sort of letter you would get from a creepy swot.

106

Dearest Dockery

I have come across some vital intelligence information, which will enable you to achieve all of your most dastardly and wicked plans. I would be most grateful if you would agree to meet me at the old oak tree near the stream in the Valley of Doom at half past ten on Saturday. I can assure you that you will be most satisfied by the outcome.

Yours sincerely
Alfie

Chapter Sixteen

THE BRILLIANT PLAN (AND A TALKING POTTY)

OK, so I guess you're desperate to find out what my plan was. You'll probably have realized by now that coming up with brilliant plans is my speciality, but this one was the most brilliant I'd ever had. In fact it was probably in the top ten most brilliant plans ever invented in the history of the world, even if I say so myself.

The thing about this brilliant plan is that it arrived in the nick of time. You see, getting massacred in the Valley of Doom, and then being kicked out of the Gang, and then temporarily joining the Dark Side, had dented my confidence, and it's hard to think up brilliant plans when your confidence is dented. But Noah's visit had changed all that. Heroes often have periods when they lose their powers and have to go off and sulk for a while. It makes the story much more exciting. Well, I'd definitely lost my powers. And, if I was being honest, I'd have to admit that I'd gone off and sulked.

But now I was back, and my powers were back, and I was ready to rock!

Perhaps the most important part of any plan is good preparation. Lots of perfectly good plans in the history of the world went wrong because of bad preparation, such as the Charge of the Light Brigade in the Crimean War. It also works the other way round (or vice-versa), such as when England won the World Cup in 1966. Well, I wanted my plan to be like winning the World Cup, and not like getting all blown to pieces in the Charge of the Light Brigade.

When preparing a good plan you need to have everything arranged in steps. The first step was writing those two cunning letters.

The second step was getting some fresh batteries for my walkie-talkies, which I'd been meaning to do for ages anyway. They each needed two AA batteries, four altogether. I dug around in my toy cupboard and got out all my old toys that used batteries, including three robots, a remote-controlled digger, a scary clown that laughed at you in a way that gave you nightmares, and a toy train that made embarrassing chuff-chuff noises.

Not a single one worked.

So then I moved on to the rest of the house. I found two batteries in my dad's electric toothbrush, which my mum got him because she said his teeth were looking green. Then I extracted (which means took out) two more from my sister Ivy's electronic potty.

According to the instructions, the potty was supposed to say 'Well done' and 'Good girl' and 'That's a big one' when you did a wee or a poo in it. But my sister's didn't work properly, and it shouted at you in Chinese, saying things like 'HONG CHOW PONG YU', which frightened her so much that she didn't go to the potty for a whole week, and had to go to hospital to get her poo extracted (which means – oh, I already explained that) by a doctor with a special kind of spoon, called a poo spoon. So taking the batteries out of it was probably the best thing you could do, and not stealing at all.

The third step was to check on the supplies of Special Mixture Number Seven. There was still some left in the bucket in the garage, but not quite enough, so I filled it up with more wee. Technically this made it Special Mixture Number Eight.

The fourth step was Noah's responsibility. He went secretly round to see everyone in the Bare Bum Gang – except of course evil Alfie – and told them the plan. No, not the whole plan, just the part they needed to know, which was where and when they had to meet up, and what to bring with them. The rest was down to me, my raw courage, and the stupidity of my mortal enemies.

Chapter Seventeen

THE TREE

I'd been up in the tree for half an hour. Half an hour is actually quite a long time to spend in a tree, even if you find a comfortable perch. Usually, when you go up into a tree, it is to get something, such as a ball that is stuck there, or perhaps your trousers, which have been thrown into the tree by a big bully, like Dockery. You don't normally hang around. Hanging around in trees is what you do if you're a monkey or a squirrel, or some other tree creature.

The tree I was in was exactly the same old oak tree I'd mentioned in the letters to Alfie and Dockery, in the deepest, darkest part of the Valley of Doom, not far at all from where we'd been ambushed. It was quite an easy tree to climb, because it had lots of branches near the ground. But I had to go fairly high up to make sure I wouldn't be seen (or heard or smelled, in case I let out a little tummy squeak).

Normally I don't like being high up in anything. It's not the heights I'm afraid of, so much as falling from them and smashing my head in. But I was on a mission, and missions are no places for scaredy cats.

So I gritted my teeth and climbed about as high up in the tree as a medium sized giraffe could reach. Giraffes can reach even further than you'd think because their tongues are as long as a killer python (or boa constrictor). Not that giraffes use their tongues for killing, unlike chameleons, and possibly some aliens who have poisonous tongues shaped like harpoons that they

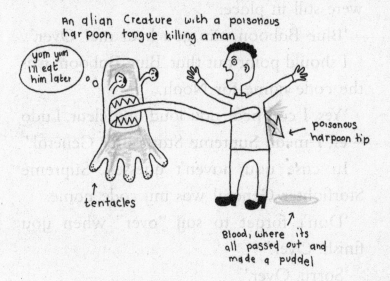

An alian Creature with a poisonous harpoon tongue killing a man

yum yum I'll eat him later

poisonous harpoon tip

tentacles

Blood, where its all passed out and made a puddel

use to paralyze you so they can eat you comfortably later on, say when they're watching telly or at a disco.

One of the main problems with trees is that they don't have toilets in them, so when you have to do a wee, you just have to sprinkle it about, willy-nilly. Actually that's quite good fun, although a bit dangerous, because it's not easy to hold on properly and wee willy-nilly at the same time.

I checked to make sure that the walkie-talkies were working, and that the Gang were still in place.

'Blue Baboon, can you hear me? Over.'

I should point out that 'Blue Baboon' was the code name for Noah.

'Yes, I can hear you loud and clear, Ludo – er, I mean Supreme Starfighter General.'

In case you haven't guessed, Supreme Starfighter General was my code name.

'Don't forget to say "over" when you finish. Over.'

'Sorry. Over.'

'Everyone in place? Over.'

'Yes, Supreme Starfighter General. Over.'

I think I heard some sniggering in the background, but it might just have been the wind in the leaves.

Noah's job had been to get the rest of them to the correct position. They were hiding in the high ground above the Valley of Doom. Noah hadn't told the Gang the whole plan. He hadn't even told them what we suspected about the evil Alfie. When you find stuff out for yourself, you learn it much better than if someone just tells you. That was the whole point of the plan – to let my friends find out for themselves how wrong they'd been.

I'd just finished my second wee (because I was bored and wanted something to do, not because I really needed one) when I heard voices.

This was it.

This is what I'd been preparing for.

The great plan was beginning.

'I wonder what that little squirt wants,'

said a loud voice I recognized at once as belonging to Dockery. I peered down through the branches, and saw four kids.

'Why don't we just punch him and steal his sweets?' said another voice.

'We had a deal, remember, and a deal's a deal, even when it's with a weasel like Alfie. Still, if I ever find out he's double-crossed us again, then he gets it.'

'Gets what?'

Then I heard the sound of a fist thumping into a palm, followed by laughter. They were right underneath me now.

Then Dockery said, 'Is it raining?'

'Don't think so, why?' replied one of the others.

'I thought I felt something drip on me.'

Whoops! That must have been the last of the wee filtering down through the leaves.

Then another voice said, 'Here he comes now. This better be good.'

It was time to get the equipment ready. I'd already tied a long piece of string round the aerial of my walkie-talkie, ready to lower it down, so that it would pick up what was said.

A walkie-talkie isn't like a phone – you can talk or you can listen, but you can't do both at the same time. To transmit you have to hold down a button when you speak. My plan was to fasten the button down with sticky tape, so it transmitted constantly. I got the tape out of my pocket and wrapped it round lots of times, so it looked like this:

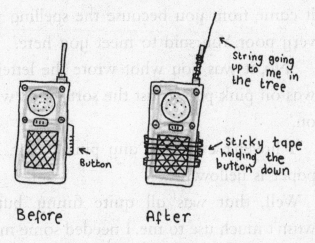

String going up to me in the tree

Sticky tape holding the button down

Button

Before   After

The walkie-talkie was now transmitting, and I hoped Noah could hear it. Very carefully I lowered it down on its string.

'Hi,' came the weak, girlie voice of Alfie.

The others grunted at him. That was their way of saying hello.

'What did you want to tell us, then?' said Dockery.

'Me?' replied Alfie. 'I thought you wanted to tell me something.'

'But you sent me a letter saying you had some vital information about those dweebs in the Bare Bum Gang.'

'No I didn't. You sent me a letter – I knew it came from you because the spelling was very poor. You said to meet you here.'

'No, it was you what wrote the letter. It was on pink paper, just the sort you'd write on.'

'I haven't even got any pink paper. My paper is yellow.'

Well, that was all quite funny, but it wasn't much use to me. I needed some more incriminating evidence.

'I don't know what you're playing

at,' growled Dockery, 'but I do know it's something sneaky. You spied for us and told us that those stupid Bare Bum kids were going to raid our den, but then you double-crossed us. For all I know you've got some other sly scheme up your sleeve.'

That was more like it!

'Just bash him,' said Larkin.

'Yeah, mash him,' said Furbank.

'No, please!' squealed Alfie. 'I'll tell you all their other secrets. I'll tell you where the traps are! I'll give you more sweets and money!'

Perfect.

'It's too late for bribery. Wait a minute – what's that?'

'What's what?'

'That dangly thing.'

'What dangly thing?'

'That dangly thing dangling there.'

It was then that I realized they were talking about the walkie-talkie. I'd let it dangle too low. Before I could pull it up,

Dockery grabbed the end and yanked. Of course I could have let go, but my walkie-talkie was my favourite toy, and I held onto my end of the string.

You can guess what happened.

I lost my balance and began to fall out of the tree.

Chapter Eighteen

DISCOVERED!

They say that before you die your life flashes before your eyes, but all that flashed before my eyes were leaves. Actually, flashes is probably the wrong word. The oak tree was so thick with leaves and twigs and branches that my fall was the slowest in history. I slid and bumped and crunched my way down until finally I found myself on the ground in a pile of dry leaves.

I looked up into the astonished faces of Alfie and the Dockery Gang. Before they had time to recover from their surprise,

I snatched the walkie-talkie from Dockery's hand, and yelled, 'NOAH, ATTACK! ATTACK NOW! GIVE THEM EVERYTHING YOU'VE GOT!'

I just hoped that they had been listening, and that Noah would understand what had happened, and what he had to do. I expected to hear them charging down the slope to my rescue, just as I'd arranged with Noah.

The group around me looked even more startled than when I'd fallen out of the tree. They glanced nervously into the bushes on either side.

But there were no war cries from the Bare Bum Gang; no charge, no rescue. I'd been abandoned. Either the walkie-talkie hadn't transmitted properly, or they hadn't heard it, or they didn't believe it, or they didn't care. My plan had failed.

Dockery laughed. 'Ha ha ha. What have we got here? Little Ludo did a bit of spying himself, did he? Hoping his friends might come and save him? Looks like he hasn't got any friends. Well, now you're going to get what every spy gets.'

Then he turned and grabbed Alfie, who'd been skulking out of the way, looking pretty miserable. 'Now I see what you were up to. In this together, eh? I never should have trusted you. Well, you get the same punishment.'

'What's that?' asked Larkin, almost panting with pleasure.

'We dunk 'em!'

The Dockery Gang roared their approval.

What he meant was that he was going to throw us in the Great Grey-Green Greasy Limpopo River. It wasn't very deep, but it was muddy and yucky and full of slime and all kinds of horrible creepy-crawlies and leeches and eels, as well as the gnats and mosquitoes and flies that buzzed over it.

A dunking in the stream was about as bad as it could get. I tried to make a run for it,

but Dockery threw his huge arm round me, and started shoving me and Alfie backwards towards the edge of the stream. The others formed a line in front of us.

'Well, Alfie,' I said, looking at him, 'we're done for now. You see what happens when you act like a sneak?'

He couldn't return my gaze, but just looked down and shuffled backwards towards the muddy stream, meekly accepting his fate.

And then I saw something that cheered me up by about eight million per cent. The Dockery Gang were facing us, shoving us towards the stream. So I could see what was happening behind them. And it was good.

Really good.

Chapter Nineteen

NOAH'S TAIL
- I MEAN TALE -
OR IS IT TAIL?
OK THEN - NOAH'S STORY

I'm about to cut to a new scene now, like
they do in the movies. I'm going to use my
imagination to pretend that I am Noah,
back about ten minutes ago, waiting up
above the Valley of Doom.

*Oh, I wonder what's happening with brave old
Ludo hiding high up in that giant oak tree (this
is meant to be Noah thinking – I'll do all
his thinking in slanty writing, so you can*

tell). *I do wish he'd call again on the walkie-talkie. Oh, how nice, a pretty birdie flying by. Ah, look, what a nice flower.*

'I'm sick of waiting here,' says Jamie.

'Me too,' says Jenny. 'And these really stink.'

She's holding out her high-powered water rifle.

But it isn't filled with water. *It's filled with Ludo's superb new Special Mixture Number Eight, the most lethal and toxic yet. We are all heavily armed. We each have two pistols and one rifle. This is all part of Ludo's brilliant plan. (I told you it was brilliant – see, even Noah agrees.)*

'I think this is all stupid,' moans The

Moan. 'In fact I think this is worse than stupid. It's plain dumb. I don't know why we're here. Ludo's been thrown out of the Gang, and we all know he'll do anything to get back in it. I reckon this is all just a big trick. And where's Alfie anyway? I know he's turned out to be a bit of a flop, but he's still in the Gang.'

'You'll see,' says Noah wisely. I mean I say, because *I'm* Noah.

Then I hear the walkie-talkie start to crackle, which means Ludo's one is transmitting.

'Listen up, everyone,' I say. 'It's beginning. Everything will become clear.'

And the others all gather closer. We all hear the sound of the walkie-talkie being lowered through the branches. And then we hear voices.

'That's Dockery,' says Jenny.

'And that's Alfie,' says Jamie.

And we hear everything they say. The whole dastardly story of deceit and lies and nastiness. I look at their faces. First they are blank, then amazed, then angry, then furious.

Then we hear the tumbling crunching sound of

poor brave Ludo falling out of the tree, and a few seconds later there's his courageous voice saying, 'Noah, attack! Attack now! Give them everything you've got.'

That makes me proud to be Ludo's second-in-command again.

Jamie and Jennifer want to charge straight down. But I say, 'Softly softly catchee monkey,' or something like that because I know lots of good sayings. So then I lead them carefully round behind the Dockery mob, keeping to the bushes and undergrowth. There is one bad moment when Jamie steps in some kind of poo – probably weasel, or possibly stoat – but he wipes it off on a handy chocolate wrapper, and we're off again.

A few metres away we spot them. Dockery, William Stanton, James Furbank, Paul Larkin, Carl Hughes, the whole gang. They have their backs to us. Ludo is facing them, looking as brave as Spider-man, Batman, Superman and Wonderwoman combined. I don't mean he looks a bit like a woman, I just mean he looks as brave as her.

Then I see something surprising. Naughty Alfie is next to Ludo. They are being pushed remorselessly back towards the terrifying torrent that is the Great Grey-Green Greasy Limpopo River. They teeter on the edge. It's now or never.

'Chaaaaaaarge!'

Chapter Twenty

THE GREAT BATTLE OF THE LIMPOPO RIVER

'Chaaaaaarge,' yelled Noah, sounding not a bit like himself.

Noah was basically the nicest boy in the world, but now he sounded like a manic Samurai warrior crossed with King Kong with a dash of rabid wolverine thrown in for good measure.

And he wasn't just shouting 'Charge', he was actually charging as well. And the rest of the Bare Bum Gang were with him, in all their magnificent glory. Jennifer was next, her face exactly like a picture of an Amazon girl warrior I'd seen in my book of legends. Then came Jamie, who, as Gang General, should probably have been leading the charge. But he wasn't a very fast runner, or a fast thinker, so he was usually better off following where others led. And last came The Moan, not moaning, but shouting his head off like the rest of them. And as they charged they let loose a volley from their heavy artillery –

the water cannons, pumped up to maximum power.

Dockery and his gang spun round at the first scream of 'Charge'. The tremendous spectacle of the attacking Bare Bum Gang made them stagger back, their faces filled with shock and awe.

Then Dockery started to laugh. 'Oh, it's only that bunch of wimps,' he said.

'Yeah,' sneered Larkin, 'with their ickle-wickle water pistols.'

'Let's bash 'em,' growled Firbank.

'And mash 'em,' added Stanton.

'This is perfect,' said Dockery. 'Like lambs to the slaughter. We can get the whole lot of them together.'

Then it hit them.

Now, the Super Soaker Aqua-Shock HydroBlitz packs a decent punch, but on its own it wouldn't take out a big oaf like Dockery. Not filled with water.

But the water cannon and pistols weren't filled with water, but Special Mixture Number Eight. I'd realized the fatal flaw in our first plan to attack the Dockery den. The delivery system, meaning the balloons, just wasn't reliable enough. But I'd fixed that now.

You could definitely smell the streams of foulness before they hit you. It was as if the smelliest tramp in the world had come and sat next to you on the bus and then rammed your nose into his armpit. No, it was worse than that, because this was wet and soaked you and there was no escaping it. It was a tidal wave of stink.

The Bare Bum Gang aimed well, zapping every one of the Dockery mob. The trouble was that Alfie and I were standing right behind them, so we also got hit, but not too badly. Even so, I nearly fainted with the foulness of it, and Alfie fell onto all fours and looked like he was going to throw up.

You can imagine how much worse it was for the Dockery Gang. They got it right in their faces, in their open mouths, in their ears. It was carnage. All you could hear were their screams and wails as they waved their hands in front of their faces in a futile attempt to fend off the deadly flood.

But Dockery wasn't quite finished yet. Bellowing like a bull, he pushed forward against the blast, using nothing but his brutish strength. Horrible though he was, I had to admire the courage of my opponent. It looked like he was going to reach Noah, whose stream from his rifle was now a dribble, before he had the chance to switch to a pistol. That would have been a disaster — if he reached Noah we'd have to surrender to save him from getting a terrible bashing.

'Here!' yelled Jenny, and threw me her spare weapon, a Max Infusion Flash Flood. I caught it in one hand, did a forward roll through the middle of the Dockery formation, spun and took careful aim.

The Flash Flood hasn't got the raw power of the HydroBlitz, but it's way more accurate. I'll let others claim it's a girl's weapon — I prefer to describe it as a precision instrument, designed for pinpoint, scientific squirting. I fired a stream straight up Dockery's nose and into his brain.

That finished him. He stopped dead in his tracks. His eyes went blank. Then he collapsed backwards, squashing two of the others.

Chapter Twenty-one

VICTORY!

'Cease fire!' I commanded.

The battle was won. Dockery and the others dragged themselves away, gagging and spluttering, wailing like babies who had lost their dummies.

The Bare Bum Gang all gathered round. They were exhausted from the fight, and they'd all suffered from the terrible stink power of Special Mixture Number Eight. There was something else in their faces as well; something that held them back from celebrating the victory.

It was Jenny who spoke first.

'We're really sorry,' she said meekly. 'We should have believed you and not him.'

She pointed to the side of the Great Grey-Green Greasy Limpopo River where Alfie was still cowering. I'd completely forgotten about him.

'Will you be our Gang Leader again, like the Olden Days?'

'Of course I will,' I said, and I couldn't stop myself from grinning. 'If that's what you all want.'

'YES!' they all shouted.

'I'm sorry too,' said Alfie, looking up at me.

'Tell us the truth, Alfie,' I said to him in a level voice. 'You spied on us and told Dockery we were coming, and which route we were taking, didn't you?'

He nodded.

'And then you rescued us, so you could look like a hero, didn't you?'

'I only wanted to be friends,' he said sadly. 'I wanted to be in your gang more than anything. And I didn't mean all that bad stuff to happen. It just all got out of control.'

'But you did steal the sweets and blame it on me, didn't you?' I asked, more sternly. 'You crammed the papers in my binocular case when we weren't looking.'

Alfie didn't answer. He just looked down, his lip started to quiver and he began to cry.

'What a horrible little creep,' sighed The Moan. 'I say we push him in the stream and throw stones at him to teach him a lesson.'

'Good idea,' said Jamie. 'Not stones, though, just mud.'

I looked at little Alfie, all pale and alone, and I felt sorry for him. It's hard moving to a new place and trying to make friends. We've all made mistakes and done things we regret.

'I don't think we should do anything horrible to him,' I said after I'd thought for a moment. 'Everyone deserves a second chance.'

'You're not going to let him in the Gang, are you?' said Jenny. 'Not after all he's done?'

'No way,' I replied. 'He can go and join the Commandos. I'll tell Declan he's OK.'

That was actually quite a cunning plan. The Commandos weren't our enemies, but they were still our rivals. I liked the idea of them having a rubbish gang member, which would make them much less cool.

You have to be clever like that when you're a Gang Leader.

Alfie stopped crying and mumbled, 'Thanks.'

'You can go now,' I said.

As he ran away, The Moan gave him a quick squirt of Special Mixture Number Eight up the backside.

'I don't know about you lot,' I said, 'but I'm going home for a bath. I smell like something that's been scraped off the floor in the zoo.'

Everyone laughed, and we set off out of the Valley of Doom.

I found myself walking next to Noah. I put my arm around his shoulders. 'Thanks,' I said. 'You were magnificent.'

He looked up at me, and I thought we were about to have some more tears, but happy ones this time. But he pulled himself together,

 remembering that crying is still mainly suitable for girls.

'Welcome back,' he said. 'Welcome back.'

Ludo's Top Ten Tips for Repelling Your Enemies

If you have a really cool den then there is a good chance it will come under attack from your enemies. If they get close enough, they will do terrible things to your den, such as utterly destroy it, wee in it, take your sweet stash, put rude graffiti in it, etc., etc. It is therefore very important to properly defend your den. I have already explained how to make brilliant traps, such as the Smarties-tube Fart Bomb trap. Here are some of the other things you could do. If you do all of them, then I guarantee no enemies will ever succeed in conquering you or your den. Plus, if the earth is ever invaded by gaseous aliens from Uranus, you will be safe inside your den, even if the rest of the planet is reduced to smouldering rubble.

1. Dig a moat. This should be at least three metres deep and should go all around your den. If you can, you should fill the moat with crocodiles, alligators, poisonous snakes, sharks, Loch Ness monsters etc. etc., which will eat, poison or scare your enemies before they have the chance to destroy you. In the Olden Days, all the toilets in a castle would empty into the moat, which would also put off people from swimming across. You probably shouldn't copy this, as someone might see you doing a wee in the moat and tell your mum or the teacher.

A really good moat

Jelly fish

man eating shark

Lock ness monster

electric eel

deadly crocodile

2 Get some old chicken bones and arrange them to look like a human skellington just outside your den. That will make your enemies think that you have a special beam that can skellify them if they attack.

3. Make an early warning system to stop your enemies sneaking up on you. Get some tin cans. Punch a hole in the bottom of each one (get a grown-up to do this if you are a wuss, or ask someone in the army who will blast lots of holes in your cans with a machine gun), then tie them together with fishing line (or your dad's shoe laces) and hide them near your den. Your enemies will get tangled up in the cans, making a terrible racket. You will then be able to counter-attack. Or run away.

4. Have a really rubbish den that no-body would want to invade or destroy. You could put little pink curtains up in it and have a dolly tea service laid out.

5. Build a dummy den a little way off from your real den. Your enemies will then destroy the pretend den and run off, whooping like baboons. You can then laugh at them for being silly fools, idiots, nincompoops, baboons, etc., etc.

6. Run away. Sometimes, if you are heavily outnumbered, or if your enemies are big and hairy, running away is a perfectly good plan and not even a bit cowardly.

7. Get a vicious guard dog, such as the one in another brilliant Bare Bum Gang story: **The Bare Bum Gang Battle the Dogsnatchers.** He is called Rude Word because his name is a rude word I'm not allowed to say.

8. Cover your den in a cloak of invisibility. Admittedly, this only works in books with wizards in them, but if you are in one of those books, then it is a good plan.

9. Find a mad scientist who will help you to develop a special ray that skellifies your enemies (see number 2 above).

10. I can't think of any more tips, which is very annoying as ten is a nice round number, and I was told I could have a pound for every one I thought up. Can you help me out?

It all started when Jennifer Eccles said she wanted to be in our gang. Until then we were just called *the Gang*...

Meet Ludo, Noah, Jamie and Phillip –
THE BARE BUM GANG!

The gang's new name is bad enough, but things are about to get much worse. Their number one enemies have challenged them to a football match, and the prize at stake is the gang den. And guess what – THEY'RE ALL COMPLETELY RUBBISH AT FOOTBALL!

How can they save the den? How can they get back their pride?

Find out in the first Bare Bum Gang adventure!

978-1-862-30386-7

Ludo, Noah, Jamie, Phillip and Jennifer are **THE BARE BUM GANG**! They have an embarrassing name but a cool Gang Den, so things could be worse.

The newest member of the gang is Rude Word, the world's ugliest dog — and he's causing trouble. He's throwing up strange furry body parts . . . and Mrs Cake's dog Trixie is missing! Ludo and the gang have to turn detective and get to the bottom of this gross mystery. But when other pets disappear, they realize the mystery is bigger than they'd thought.

Can they get Rude Word off the hook?

978-1-862-30387-4

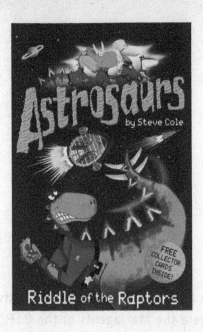

Riddle of the Raptors

Teggs is no ordinary dinosaur – he's an
ASTROSAUR! Captain of the amazing
spaceship DSS *Sauropod*, he goes on dangerous
missions and fights evil – along with his faithful
crew, Gypsy, Arx and Iggy!

When a greedy gang of meat-eating raptors raid
the *Sauropod* and kidnap two top athletes, Teggs
and his crew race to the rescue. But there's more
to the raptors' plot than meets the eye.

Can Teggs solve their rascally riddle in time?

978-0-099-47294-0

Genius cow Professor McMoo and his trusty sidekicks,
Pat and Bo, are the star agents of the C.I.A. – short for
COWS IN ACTION! They travel through time, fighting evil
bulls from the future and keeping history on the right
track. . .

When Professor McMoo invents a brilliant TIME
MACHINE, he and his friends are soon attacked by a
terrifying TER-MOO-NATOR – a deadly robo-cow who
wants to mess with the past and change the future!
And that's only the start of an incredible ADVENTURE
that takes McMoo, Pat and Bo from a cow paradise in
the future to the SCARY dungeons of King Henry VIII. . .

IT'S TIME FOR ACTION. COWS IN ACTION!

978-1-862-30189-4

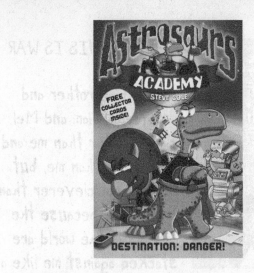

Young Teggs Stegosaur is a pupil at
ASTROSAURS ACADEMY – where dinosaurs
train to be ASTROSAURS. With his best friends
Blink and Dutch beside him, amazing adventures
and far-out fun are never far away!

Arriving at the academy, the new astro-
cadets face their first mission – to camp out
in a deserted space wilderness and bring back
something exciting for show-and-tell. But the
sneaky tricks of a rival team mean big trouble
for Teggs, Blink and Dutch – especially when
a T.rex ship crash-lands close by with a VERY
hungry crew. . .

978-1-862-30553-3

BONSAI! THIS IS WAR

My big brother and sister, William and Mel, may be older than me and biggerer than me, but they're not cleverer than me. Just because the chips of the world are stacked against me like a potato mountain doesn't mean they can beat me. Revenge will be mine!

Or rather mine and the Revengers, and a boa constrictor called Alfred's. Let loose the snakes of doom and see how they like it then! I shall have my revenge before you can say 'peanut butter and jam sandwiches'! Actually I shouldn't have mentioned peanut butter and jam sandwiches. Forget you ever read that. If you don't, I may have to kill you.

The first book in a brilliant and hilarious series by award-winning comic writer, Jamie Rix.

9780440864769